I Dreamt About It

I Dreamt About It

Yastika Singh

ARCHWAY
PUBLISHING

Archway Publishing books may be ordered
through booksellers or by contacting:

Archway Publishing
1663 Liberty Drive
Bloomington, IN 47403
www.archwaypublishing.com
1 (888) 242-5904

ISBN: 978-1-4808-2978-7 (sc)
ISBN: 978-1-4808-2979-4 (e)

Library of Congress Control Number: 2016905199

Print information available on the last page.

Archway Publishing rev. date: 4/22/2016

Series Title

Also by Yastika Singh

Random Harvest – a collection of 5 short stories with morals. It is perfect as a read-along with young kids and is available as an e-book on Amazon.com.

Dedication

For my mom, dad and sister

For encouraging me and for always being there for me, for letting me dream big...

Epigraph

If you can dream it, you can do it.

By Walt Disney

Contents

Preface

What are your hobbies? What do you like to do in your free time? Everyone will have different answers to these questions. This book is filled with stories about realistic characters. They find some challenges when they are pursuing their dreams and those challenges turn into adventures. The main character in every story learns a life lesson which makes them stronger. Some lack confidence, some are just too shy. Whatever it is, they're just like you and me. They learn some amazing things and have amazing times while doing so with a touch of magic. I got my inspiration to write this book by living my normal life. It's true! My stories are based on things I do in my free time. I play chess, I do gymnastics, and of course I love to write. I hope you enjoy this book. And remember. Don't be afraid to follow your dreams!

First Female President

Chapter 1: The Journey Begins

Sometimes I wish I hadn't dropped out of the elections. Sometimes I wish I hadn't just stood there, frozen, listening to all the nonsense people were shouting at me. My name is Quail Lortano and I am the first female president of the United States. I am going to tell you about what I learned from my past.

I was born on November 17, 1940, and I grew up on a small farm in Kansas. My parents were poor farmers and I was an only child. I went to school at Crystal Springs School. Since childhood, I was very attached to animals. I talked to them, listened to them, and played with them. I was very happy to live on a farm. I also used to dream of becoming president. I read books about the White House and what a president's job was. I learned a lot from these books and by the time I was twenty, I felt that I knew everything about running a country. I wanted to go to college but I knew that I would need more money to do so. I got a job in a coffee shop and worked long hours to make my dream come true. Every morning, I started at 6:00 a.m. and got home at 10:00 p.m. Finally, I had enough money to go to college. Wichita State University was my only option because it was the closest. So I left for the university on August 17, 1960. The leadership course and the animal-science course were my favorites. I learned a lot and in 1963, I graduated from college. I was ready for the real world.

I already had a plan for my life. I would work as a zookeeper, and in my spare time, I would write speeches and come up with ways to run a country. I really loved my life as I got to be with animals and practice being a leader. On weekends, I spent time working on an invention. It was a small device that you could put on animals. When you pressed a button, it would give the animal a shower. When I finished the design, I sold a few of the devices to nearby pet stores. They really liked my invention. Soon enough, I was a millionaire with my own company called *Paw-tific Showers*. Twelve years after I left college, I was thirty-five years old and I considered this to be my best birthday. Why? I was finally eligible to run for president! Since I had come up with many speeches before, I started making speeches in public.

Chapter 2: Trouble

That is when the trouble started. On September 7, 1976, I had made my eighth speech. A man with pink sunglasses in the front row called out, "Hey! Women can't run for president! They are supposed to be taking care of the children and cooking and cleaning the house."

Other men started shouting at me in agreement and it was very upsetting. I stood there, just frozen. I couldn't say anything and I couldn't move. My heart was beating so loudly that I could hear it. Then I did something horrible. I let them bully me. I was a little mouse surrounded by a dozen cats. They were poisoning my mind that I had no right to be a president. I ran away.

For five years, I stayed at home. Only when I needed to go grocery shopping did I go outside and even then, I did so in disguise. I was too ashamed to show my face even to my parents. I was ashamed for two reasons: One, I had made a bad example of a woman standing up for herself, and two, I was actually winning, but because I had dropped out of the elections, I didn't qualify. Then something wonderful happened.

Chapter 3: My Comeback

One morning I woke up at 5:00 a.m. I heard birds chirping beautifully. The sound of animals was irresistible to me because I had been away from my zookeeper job for a long time. I went outside to find the talented birds and I saw something terrible occur. A big bird had pushed a little bird away and the little bird looked hurt. Just when I thought that this was a disaster, the other birds started singing. Suddenly, the little bird joined the singing. The big bird pushed the little bird again. But the little bird just kept on singing. That is when I understood: He didn't let the big bird bully him. I realized that I shouldn't have let "Mr. Pink Glasses" bully me. I shouldn't have listened to him; I should have believed in myself.

For three years I came up with even more powerful speeches. I made a special speech about equality. I wanted to show "Mr. Pink Glasses" that women were as good as men. I wanted to make a comeback.

On June 23, 1984, I decided to run for president again. I was ready to make it happen. On July 1, 1984, I made my first speech, a special one about equality. I got to the podium, a little bit nervous. Suddenly, there was dead silence. I mustered up my courage and started to speak.

It started out pretty rough. People were shouting

Yastika Singh

things like, "Hey! It's Lortano! She gonna be a moving statue again?" I suddenly felt a little overwhelmed. *What if they didn't listen to me? What if they just laughed? What if no one voted for me?* I thought. Then a surge of energy burst through my body. I took a deep breath. After I started blocking the protesters out of my mind, things went as smooth as a calm river. "I was a victim of bullying, but now, I will rise up and prove that I am just as good as anyone. Everyone is equal. I know I can run this country. I do not care if none of you vote for me; I know I am capable of running America. I will do all I can to improve this country. And discrimination will never be tolerated. Thank you." I got a standing ovation. I was amazed. I never knew one little speech could change such a big mistake. I had meant every word of my speech. I really, really wanted to help America.

I was very excited. I made many other speeches without trouble and now it was election time. So on November 3, I sat on my couch and tuned to Channel 12, that was covering the election. A man with black hair was announcing, "Ten, nine, eight, seven, six, five…" I crossed my fingers. "…four, three, two, one…the next president of the United States is …Tom Lar…..oh no…sorry! The next president of the United States is ….Quail Lortano!"

I squealed with joy. I jumped on my couch until I was tired. I couldn't believe my dream had come true. It all happened so fast, maybe a little too fast.

Just then, the paparazzi showed up and they tried to break open the door. They burst in all at once. I had expected that something like this would happen, but it still took me by surprise. Then something happened that I had not expected at all: Tom Larcy walked in the door. He was my closest rival. I figured he was mad that I had won, so I stood there like a statue. But I was actually surprised at his reaction.

"Quail," he said, "I came to congratulate you. You have worked very hard for this, and I am very happy for you".

I was taken aback and something told me that he was not telling the truth. Anyway, I accepted his praise gracefully. All the while, the paparazzi were flashing their cameras at me. Then I got a phone call from Doo McDay, the head reporter of the *Washington Gazette*. He wanted to interview me. He invited me to Washington, D.C. on Wednesday. Elated, I packed my bags and started to think about all the possible questions that might come up during the interview.

On Tuesday morning, I went to the airport. I was amazed at how many people let me cut in line for security! A businessman who struck up a conversation with me soon offered to let me take his private jet to Washington, D.C. How could I turn down an offer like that? So I thanked him and waited on the side of the line to be escorted to the jet.

Then I saw my luxurious ride. There were red velvet seats, gold embroidered windows, and movie screens with just about every American movie! I couldn't believe my eyes. The best part about my special trip was that we left right away. I slept most of the time. When I woke up, I saw bright white buildings and streets lined with cherry trees. The pilot taxied onto the runway of the private airstrip. The pilot saluted me and I saluted back. I stepped out of the plane and looked at the city around me. It was 4:00 p.m. and also the start of an amazing new life.

Chapter 4: Bird Speech

That is what I had thought my day would be like, but in reality, it wasn't very "amazing" at all. Once I got out of the airport, I got into a taxi and asked the driver to drive me to my hotel, *The President*. When I reached there, I paid the driver and got out with my luggage. I checked in, got my key, went to my room, and flopped on my bed. After that, I had dinner and got ready to retire.

The next morning, I was woken up by my animal sounds alarm clock. When I opened my eyes, I was blinded by the sunlight. After lazing for a while, I finally stumbled out of my bed. I realized that it was the day of my interview. I quickly got ready and ordered a magnificent breakfast of pancakes and fruit. After I ate the last piece of fruit, I grabbed my papers and ran to the door. I found a letter stuck under the door. I stepped out of the hotel and hailed a taxi. As soon as I got in, the driver announced loudly, "Look, everyone. It is the president-elect". I quickly closed the door. The taxi raced through the streets of Washington, D.C. When we reached the offices of the *Washington Gazette*, the driver said, "The ride is free". I gave him a 10-dollar bill anyway. As I stepped out of the taxi, a group of reporters swarmed around me. They started asking a lot of questions. With so many microphones in front of me, I couldn't take even one step forward. "Excuse me, please. I will be happy to answer all your questions after my scheduled interview!" Eventually, they let me through. I walked by a beautiful lawn in front of the building. I showed the guard my invitation and he let me in. I was impressed with the security in the building. A few minutes later, I was seated across from Doo McDay, who started the interview by asking me about my experience running for president. There were lots of people in the room and the lights and camera were focused on Doo McDay and me.

"The first time I ran for president, I dropped out because someone insulted me. Five years later, I found inspiration to run again right in my backyard. I know it sounds crazy, but it is true. I saw a big bird push a little bird away and the little bird seemed hurt. Seeing this, a group of birds started singing and the little bird started singing along. The big bird kept pushing, but the little bird continued singing. That was three years ago. Now, here I am. I would like to thank whoever insulted me because I have learnt a lot from this experience."

Someone in the room suddenly shouted, "What a psycho! Inspired by birds! Is this the kind of president we want?" There was silence. Then, someone spoke up. "That was a great story, Ms. Lortano!", he said, and started clapping. Soon, everyone in the room joined in. The man who had called me a psycho quietly slipped out of the room.

Chapter 5: The Oath

My swearing-in ceremony was held on January 21, 1985 (since January 20, 1985 was a Sunday). It was a memorable day for me. I took my oath, feeling excited and confident. The applause from the crowd in front of the Capitol seemed to go on forever. I was ready to change America. I was ready to change people's lives.

<u>GOD BLESS AMERICA!!!</u>

The Game Setup

Chapter 1: A Loss and a Birthday

"Why are the pawns in front?" Pearl Shoelock thought as she walked into the tournament room. She was in section four (USCF rating under twelve hundred), and was supposed to play white at table number three. She waited nervously for her opponent. Just then, a tall boy sat down opposite her. His hair was parted carefully and had lots of gel, making it look slick and shiny. Pearl gulped. She felt sick. She had had this feeling many times before, when she had to play against boys in chess tournaments. She was convinced that boys would beat her even before the games started. Pearl started to sweat. A bugle sounded, indicating that players should start their games. Everyone in the room shook hands with their opponents. "You're going down!" the tall boy whispered. Pearl tried to concentrate on the board but couldn't. Tears swelled up in her eyes. They had only played for five minutes when the boy said triumphantly, "Checkmate!" Pearl stared at the board, not able to register the fact that she had lost in five minutes. Slowly, she shook hands with the boy and got up from her chair. She realized that she had let the boy's words affect her game. She had lost the game even before they started playing.

After the tournament, Pearl went home feeling very sad. She had lost two other games and had won just one. When her parents asked her why she had lost, Pearl knew the answer. Pearl thought about what happened while her mother was making dinner. At the dinner table, Pearl barely touched her food. Her sister, Violet, tried to cheer her up but Pearl was too ashamed to speak. She didn't feel like talking to anyone, so she went to bed early.

A few days later, it was Pearl's twelfth birthday. She woke up early to make the most of her special day. At the breakfast table, her father asked, "Pearl, there is a huge tournament on Sunday. Would you like to go?"

Pearl gulped. "Sure!" she said, trying to sound excited. She was sure she would lose all her games. When it was time for Pearl to open her presents, she sat down in the middle of the tiled kitchen floor. She opened a small box that had bright green wrapping paper, and found sparkling gold earrings inside. This was Violet's gift.

"Oh, my God, thank you!" Pearl gasped.

"You're welcome. Happy birthday!" said Violet.

Pearl picked a medium sized box with dark blue wrapping paper next, to find an Agatha Christie mystery book inside. Pearl had wanted one of these books since she was seven.

"Thank you!" Pearl exclaimed.

"You're welcome. Happy birthday!" her father said.

Finally, Pearl was down to her last present. It was a large box with light pink wrapping paper. She took a deep breath and tore the wrapping paper off. She gasped as she saw what was before her eyes. Inside was a maple wood box with crowns, lions, and spears engraved in gold on the sides. The wood was smooth and smelt like burning embers. Pearl slowly opened a heavy brass latch and saw chess pieces inside. As she looked closer, she saw the kings holding tiny swords and the brave knights with their horses striking a pose on their two back legs. Every piece was designed with great detail.

"Thank you sooooo much, Mom!!!" whispered Pearl hugging her mom tightly.

"You're welcome, Pearl! I bought it at that rare antique shop downtown. Mr. Monique, the owner, thought that you would like it. You should visit him sometime. I think you'll like him." Pearl was in a daze. Something felt magical about the box.

"Ready for a game of chess?" her father asked.

"Sure!!" Pearl said enthusiastically.

Pearl's mother laughed. "Okay, you two go and play while Violet and I fix dinner."

Chapter 2: The Magic Begins

Pearl carefully carried the maple wood box to her room and set it down on her bed. Pearl and her father took out the pieces one by one, admiring their beauty each time. Finally, when all the pieces were on the board, Pearl and her father shook hands. Pearl was white[1]. She touched the center pawn[2] and placed it on the e4 square.

A chess board is like a grid. There are rows and columns. The rows are identified by numbers from 1 to 8. The columns are identified by letters from "a" to "h". To identify a square, you look at what row and what column the square is in.

Suddenly, Pearl felt her hand being pushed away. Before her father could play, a black pawn from his side moved to the e5 square by itself! Pearl and her father stared open-mouthed. As they watched, the other pieces started to move. They took turns, white, black, white, black. After a few minutes, the pieces started to talk!

The white king[3] started talking first in a deep voice. "Right knight,[4] step outside. Right bishop,[5] prepare for a Giuoco Piano[6].

---

[1] In chess, there are white pieces and there are black pieces. One player moves the white pieces and the other player moves the black pieces.

[2] A pawn is a chess piece. Each player has 8 pawns at the start of the game. Pawns are sometimes called soldiers.

[3] A king is a chess piece.

[4] A knight is a chess piece. It is sometimes called a horse.

[5] A bishop is a chess piece. It is sometimes called a camel.

[6] Giucco Piano is the name given to a popular opening in chess. It is also called the Italian Game.

Right rook,[7] prepare to castle[8]. Charge!" Pearl and her father were astounded.

"What about me, Your Majesty?" a pawn with a very high voice asked.

"Sit tight and do nothing. You are just a little pawn!" said the king. And with that he chuckled and went back to giving orders.

All this while, the black pieces were secretly making plans of their own. They were preparing to surprise the white pieces. Both sides started advancing across the board. The game grew intense. The queens[9] were exchanged very early, and soon, most of the pieces were off the board and only a few pieces and the kings remained. Black had an extra knight to his advantage. Both sides wanted to promote their pawns so that they could get a queen. White's king was able to capture a few pawns but black was capturing more of his pawns. White had an advantage, though. The pawn that had been snubbed by the king at the beginning of the game had secretly and carefully advanced to the third last row of the board. He had two more squares and then he would be at the end of the board and eligible to turn into a queen. Black played a clever move, threatening to make a queen in three moves. The white pawn continued to advance across the board. There was just one square to go now. Black gave a check to white's king, forcing him to hold off on promoting a pawn. White's king moved to the last row. Black's pawn advanced, his king protecting him. With the next move, white's pawn became a queen! It was also a check[10] on the

---

[7] A rook is a chess piece. It is also called an elephant.

[8] Castling is a way of protecting the king in chess.

[9] A queen is a chess piece. It is sometimes called a minister. It is the most powerful piece on the board.

[10] A check is another way of saying that the opponent's king is under attack.

black king, so black moved his king away. A few moves later, white had given checkmate[11] and the game was over.

"I am very proud of the way you stealthily became a queen. Very well done!" the king congratulated the pawn. "I am sorry I underestimated you." he added.

"It is all right." the pawn said modestly.

Then, all at once, the pieces went back to their starting positions. Pearl and her father were flabbergasted! They were about to talk about what had happened, when Mrs. Shoelock, called them to dinner. "We must not tell anyone about this until we are sure it is real." Pearl's father advised. Pearl nodded in agreement. They ran to the kitchen.

While slowly eating her dinner, Pearl kept thinking about the magical board. She walked thoughtfully to her bedroom and got ready to go to bed way before her usual bedtime. As she lay in bed she suddenly got scared. "What if they grow bigger and eat us all?" she wondered. She told herself that everything would be fine. She also decided that she would pay a visit to Mr. Monique, the antique dealer.

---

[11] A checkmate means one player has won. The opponent's king is under attack and it cannot escape.

Chapter 3: Explanations and Tea

The next morning, Pearl got ready to go to Mr. Monique's antique shop. "Mom, can you take me downtown to visit Mr. Monique's antique shop?" Pearl asked as she ate her Saturday morning breakfast special.

"Well, I would like to do some shopping. All right, I'll take you but not now. We'll go around 4:00 p.m." Pearl's mother said. Pearl was disappointed that they could not go right away but she decided to be patient. She waited desperately for 4:00 p.m. She read a book, watched TV, and took a shower. Finally, it was 4:00 p.m. Pearl dressed formally, thinking the old man wouldn't like the idea of a T-shirt and shorts. Pearl and her mom set out in their black Chrysler Town & Country to the antique shop.

"I will drop you at Mr. Monique's store and then I'll go shopping for some clothes. I'll pick you up at 5:00 p.m." Pearl's mother said.

"Okay!" Pearl said absent-mindedly. She was too busy thinking about what Mr. Monique would say about the magic board. After a few minutes, they reached the downtown area. Pearl spotted Mr. Monique's small store and jumped out of the car as soon as her mother stopped the car.

"Bye, Mom!" Pearl cried as she ran to the store. She stopped running right before she entered the store. Pearl pushed open the door and a small elf in a cuckoo clock sprang out and started whistling a beautiful tune.

"Why, hello there! I'm Mr. Monique," a delicate voice greeted Pearl. A man with a distinct hunch stood behind a granite counter.

"Hi! I'm Pearl Shoelock. I came to ask you about a chess board my mom bought for me. Well, it's...... let's just say it's a bit unusual."

There was a twinkle in the man's eyes. He said with a smile, "Ah, unusual, huh? If you can, please explain this chess board. I think I know which board it is and I may be able to explain a few things."

Pearl started explaining. "Well, I set up all the pieces, ready to play with my dad yesterday. I was white and I started with the classic e4 move and suddenly the pieces started to move by themselves and talk! My dad and I didn't tell anyone because we were afraid that we were seeing things. I feel like the chess board was trying to give me a message."

Mr. Monique chuckled. "It was trying to give you a message all right, but you didn't understand. Come, have tea with me and I will explain everything." The old man led Pearl to a room behind a curtain. A table was set with a pot of tea, scones, butter, and sugar cookies. They sat in wooden chairs and had their tea and snacks while Mr. Monique told Pearl about the mysterious board. "Now, as I was saying, the board was trying to give you a message. If you tell me what the pieces were saying to each other, I can tell you what the message was. See, you must read between the lines." Mr. Monique said.

Pearl closed her eyes and thought hard. "I remember that the king was giving orders to everyone. A pawn asked the king what he could do and the king laughed at him and said he was just a pawn and could do nothing. The pawn got promoted to a queen and the king took back his words and apologized." Pearl finished telling Mr. Monique everything she remembered and slowly opened her eyes.

Mr. Monique touched his chin. "I think I know the message!" he suddenly exclaimed. "You see, the box will give a different message to every person depending on their weaknesses. It will tell the person with white pieces how to overcome their weakness. The person has to decode the message. Your message is that you have to believe in yourself and not let what other people say hurt you. You must also have confidence in yourself." Mr. Monique said triumphantly.

Pearl looked puzzled. She said, "I still don't understand how you figured all that out?"

Mr. Monique chuckled. "Now that's detective work. Your story told me everything. The pawn had confidence in himself, so he did not let the king's words affect him. He kept advancing and got promoted to a queen. Most importantly, he didn't talk back to the king. He proved his point silently without making a scene. Everyone underestimated him because he was a pawn so he used that to his advantage. Now do you understand?" Mr. Monique asked Pearl.

Pearl nodded. "Yes. Thank you so much, Mr. Monique. Now that you have explained the message, I understand why it was for me. You see, I get nervous when I play boys in chess tournaments. I lose even before I start playing. Sometimes, they say discouraging things and I, well... I get discouraged. Now I understand what goes on during the tournaments. Since I am a girl, people underestimate my ability to play chess. So all I have to do is ignore the comments, have confidence, and subtly win!" Pearl said. She glanced at her watch. "Mr. Monique it is 4:55 p.m.! My mother is going to pick me up at 5:00 p.m. Thank you so much." Pearl got up from her chair ready to go.

"Goodbye, Pearl! Use what you learned from the board. And one more thing, if you see someone in need of magic, pass this tradition on. Explain the rules and give them one day to figure it out. Then take it back." Mr. Monique smiled broadly.

"I will!" Pearl promised. A car honked outside of the store. "Bye!!!" Pearl screamed as she ran to their car.

Chapter 4: The New Winner

It was Sunday, the day of the tournament. Pearl had studied hard for the tournament, learning new strategies and playing chess online. There was a particular strategy she had practiced a lot. She had brought the magic board with her just in case. When she sat down for her first game, a tall boy with gelled, carefully parted hair sat down in front of Pearl. The boy from the last tournament! But this time Pearl didn't gulp. The bugle sounded. Everyone shook hands and the games began. Pearl and the boy played for five minutes. "Checkmate!" Pearl declared. The boy sat there unable to register the fact that he had lost in five minutes. Slowly, he shook hands with Pearl and rose from his chair. Pearl was amazed, too. Mr. Monique's advice had worked. She ran to her family and told them about her win.

A few hours later, the tournament was over. Pearl had won all her games! She won first place and was awarded a trophy. Pearl suddenly remembered something. She quickly grabbed the magic board and walked up to the tall boy. "This is a magic board. It helped me build my confidence. I don't know what it will do for you but try it. I know it sounds crazy but give it a shot. Please return it tomorrow, though." She told him. She took out a piece of paper and pencil, scribbled her address on it, and handed it to the boy. "Goodbye!" She said. And with that she ran to her family.

"How come you were so confident this time?" Pearl's mom asked her in their car.

"Let's just say I have the magic touch."

The next morning, there was a knock on the Shoelocks' door. Pearl opened the door. The tall boy from the tournament was standing in front of her. He was holding the magic board. "Thank you. I learned that I was overconfident. This board helped me a lot. I'm sorry I underestimated you." He said.

"You're welcome and its okay." Pearl said and took the box. "Bye." She said. As she closed the door, she remembered the question she had asked herself before the last tournament. Now, she knew the answer. "Pawns are in front because they are the smallest but cleverest warriors of them all."

CHECKMATE!!!

All For a Medal's Sake

Chapter I: A Wrong Turn

Bonto Lansing grinned as Mayor Roberto placed a shining bronze medal around his neck. Bonto had been waiting for this moment all his life. And to think that it all started with the New Jersey State Cross Country Championships…

Bonto stretched his legs. He was at the starting point of the New Jersey State Cross Country Championship race course. The fourteen year old boy had moved to New Jersey from Montana just two months before because his father had found a new job. Bonto had been a star in his cross country team back in Montana and was expected to win lots of medals. But, his family had moved to New Jersey before he ran a single race in Montana. So, Bonto joined the school cross country team in New Jersey. Bonto had one dream. He wanted to win a shiny gold medal. The NJSCCC was his best shot to do so. Bonto had been shown the race route many times but he was still not comfortable with running on his own. Suddenly, he heard a man announce on a megaphone, "The race will now begin in three, two, one! Boom!" the starting pistol went off. Bonto and the other runners accelerated down the path, running at 9 miles an hour. Bonto looked back to see that he had passed all the runners. He breezed past trees and streams. He bore right at a fork. A couple of minutes later, everyone else bore left.

After a few minutes, Bonto had a feeling that something was wrong. He stopped and looked around. There was nobody in sight. He wondered where all the other runners were. He couldn't hear the constant huffing and puffing and steady footsteps of the runners. Suddenly, it occurred to him that he was lost. In his panic, he could not remember how

Yastika Singh

he had got there. He tried to remember as best as he could but to no avail. Bonto decided to keep running straight, hoping to reach a town. He started his journey through the woods. Bonto was very tired but he kept running. At last, a bit of sunshine flooded through the woods. Bonto could see a town through the trees. From a sign posted at the edge of the town, he understood that it was called Day Park. He sprinted out of the woods, feeling hopeful.

Chapter 2: The Bejeweled Scissors

Meanwhile, while Bonto was still running through the woods, a grand opening of Day Park's newest jewelry store, *Shining Diamond*, was being held at the far side of the town. A crowd had gathered around a red carpet to watch the ceremony. The mayor was supposed to cut the ribbon with a giant, bejeweled scissors. The bejeweled scissors was on display on a decorative stand. The owner, Frank De'mone, was too busy giving commands about the banquet that was to be held after the ceremony to notice that a masked thief had come and was eyeing the jeweled scissors. As quick as a cat, the thief picked up the scissors and raced away as quickly as he had come. When Frank De'Mone turned around, he gasped at the empty stand and screamed out commands to find the thief.

As the masked man hurdled through Day Park, he thought about what to do with the scissors. Maybe he would sell it for tons of money. Maybe he would ask Frank De'Mone for a lot of money in return for the scissors. He decided no matter what he did with the scissors, money would pour into his hands. He remembered the reason why he stole things. He was too ashamed to even think about why he wanted the money so badly. Suddenly, his thoughts were interrupted as Bonto came running towards him, unable to stop. Crash! They both came crashing down on top of each other. Bonto quickly looked at the man's mask, guessed he was a thief, and took the scissors away from his grasp. He held the thief down by sitting on him.

He then took out one of his shoelaces and tied the thief's hands together. "Where did you get these scissors?" Bonto asked.

"The grand opening of the *Shining Diamond*" the robber grumbled.

"Take me to it." Bonto ordered. The thief hesitated, but not seeing any way to escape, he led Bonto to the *Shining Diamond*.

Chapter 3: Cutting of the Ribbon

When Bonto and the thief arrived at the *Shining Diamond* with the bejeweled scissors, the crowd cheered. Two policemen started to take the thief away but Bonto stopped them. "Please finish the ceremony first. I would like to then speak to him alone." he said. So the ceremony began. Frank De`Mone gave a small speech about how honored he was to own a shop in "such a lovely town". Then it was time to cut the red ribbon. Frank De`Mone asked Bonto to cut it. Bonto was honored. He took a step forward, scissors in hand, and then stopped. "Why not put on a show while I'm at it?" he thought. Bonto came running at the ribbon and cut it just in time for him to run through it. Everyone clapped and cheered.

Yastika Singh

A few minutes later, when the banquet started, Bonto asked to talk with the thief alone. Bonto began. "What is your name?"

"Mark Dollty" the thief replied.

"Why did you steal the scissors? Why do you want the money?" Bonto questioned.

"Why do I have to answer these questions? Why can't you just leave me alone and let me go to jail? It's not like I'll ever be rich enough to go to college!" the thief shouted. He suddenly covered his mouth, as if he had given away a secret.

Bonto stood in shock. He quickly recovered and turned back to Mark. "You could have just told me. You can take a loan, can't you?" Bonto said softly.

Mark Dollty stood in silence. "How would I ever pay it back? All I ever wanted was to go to college. Then my parents died. Now I only have our house." Mark explained.

Bonto had an idea. "If you promise to never steal anything again, I may be able to convince Frank De'Mone to let you get a job at the *Shining Diamond* to pay for your college."

Mark looked up. "Oh yes, yes, yes!!! I won't steal anything ever again. Thank you so much!!!" Mark started jumping up and down.

Chapter 4: Medal of Honor

An hour later, when the banquet was over, the mayor of the town asked Bonto to come up to him. Bonto did as he was told.

"What is your name, kid?" Mayor Roberto asked.

"Bonto Lansing, sir", Bonto replied.

The Mayor placed a medal of honor on Bonto's neck for recovering the bejeweled scissors. Everyone applauded. "Is there anything Day Park can do for you?" Mayor Roberto asked Bonto.

"Well, there are two things that I would like – First, please let Mark Dollty work at the *Shining Diamond*. He promised to never steal anything again. He needs the money to go to college. It is his dream. Second, I need a ride to the NJSCCC because I got lost during the race and stumbled into Day Park."

Mayor Roberto was deep in thought. "Okay, I will fulfil these wishes. But, if Mark steals anything, I will hold you responsible!"

Bonto looked at Mark Dollty. After a moment, Bonto said, "Okay, I agree."

Soon it was time for Bonto to leave. Everyone cheered for him. Mark Dollty looked him in the eye and said, "I won't let you down."

"I know you won't." Bonto replied. Soon the mayor's car pulled away from Day Park. Bonto waved to everyone.

When Mayor Roberto and Bonto reached the NJSCCC, Bonto got out of the car and waved to him. Mayor Roberto waved back at Bonto and then pulled away. Bonto ran over to his team. They were relieved to see him safe. He explained to them what had happened. Soon it was time for everyone to leave. Bonto's team hadn't won but they had had fun.

Chapter 5: A Great Ending

Back in Day Park, Mark Dollty had started his work at the *Shining Diamond*. At 5:00 p.m., he got his first paycheck. He thought about Bonto and how he had helped Mark. Mark knew that thanks to Bonto, he would have a great future.

Five years later, Bonto had a full show case of running medals. He could still remember the day when he had hung up his very first medal. It was his favorite one, The Medal of Honor. Whenever Bonto looked at it, he remembered his adventures in Day Park, and also how he had helped someone in need.

<u>KEEP ON RUNNING!!!</u>

The Nun's Secret Door

Chapter 1: "You Are Late!"

Sylvia slipped through the secret door quietly and pushed the bookshelf in front of it. She sighed contentedly and thought about the small creatures and forests in her stories. Squirrels scampering, snakes slithering, butterflies fluttering….. "Sylvia!" a shrill voice rang out. Mother Hope stepped into the small gift shop just as Sylvia finished pushing the bookshelf. The St. Stephen's Nunnery is a nunnery as well as a tourist attraction. People tour the nunnery, watch the nuns in action, and buy souvenirs from the gift shop. It is located in the Majestic Rocks in Greece.

"Sylvia! You are late for your evening prayers! You are leading today! Come on!"

Sylvia hurriedly said, "Sorry! I will be there!" She followed the stomping Mother Hope to the prayer room and started the evening prayers.

When the prayers were over, Mother Hope dismissed everyone except Sylvia. "You will come to my office." Sylvia followed Mother Hope and sat down on one of the red velvet chairs. Mother Hope took her seat.

She cleared her throat and started to speak. "Sylvia, it is none of my business as to what you are doing but I can't keep waiting for you all the time. You are missing out on prayers and that is not acceptable."

Sylvia shuffled and said, "But, Mother Hope! I was doing something very important".

"Is it too important to tell me?" Mother Hope challenged. Sylvia fell silent. "Look, Sylvia, you are on thin ice. I suggest you take your duties seriously. You are dismissed." Mother Hope held her head high.

"Yes, Mother Hope." Sylvia muttered. She rose from her seat and went to her room.

Chapter 2: Nightly Visit

As the clock in the hall struck midnight, Sylvia jumped out of her bed. It was time for her nightly visit to her secret place. She tiptoed down the dark hall and down the creaky stairs. Sylvia knew that all the nuns were sound sleepers but she did not want to take any chances. She tiptoed to the gift shop and pushed aside the bookshelf. She stood before a wide, old oak door. It had a brass knob and beautiful carvings in the wood. She turned the knob and pushed the door open. Sylvia entered a huge room with bright green walls. In the center of the room there was a rectangular table with papers, pens, and a container with white paint. To the left of this table was another table with paints of various colors, leather, and a sewing kit. To the right was a bookshelf filled with handmade books that Sylvia had made. Tonight Sylvia wanted to add another book to the shelf. So, she got to work. She got out a matchbox and lit two candles that were on the center table. Then, she started to read a stack of papers that were on the table. She used white paint to paint over words that she wanted to erase or change. She then walked over to the table with the various colors. Sylvia painted colorful pictures that were related to her story. When the paint had dried, Sylvia placed the pictures in the stack of papers in the right places to match her story. Next, Sylvia made her book cover out of leather. She painted the title of her book, "The Mysterious Lodge", a picture of a wolf and a wooden lodge, and her name, Sylvia Mint, on the book cover. Lastly, she sewed the leather and the pages together. The book was ready. It was about the legend of a mysterious lodge and how the legend was actually true. Sylvia sighed and studied her work of art. Satisfied, she put it on the bookshelf. She suddenly yawned and realized that she was very tired. She blew out the candles and tiptoed out the door. She pushed the bookshelf back and silently walked back to her room and fell asleep.

Chapter 3: The Little Girl

The next morning, Sylvia woke up at 7:00 a.m., much after the other nuns woke up. She brushed her teeth, took a quick shower, got dressed, and bustled down the stairs. Sylvia was expecting a very busy day. It was the one day of the week when tourists came. Sylvia and a group of other nuns were on cleaning duty. Sylvia was to dust the rooms. It was her least favorite job. She sneezed the whole time she was dusting. Finally, she was done. Sylvia changed out of her cleaning clothes just in time to see the first tourists arriving. She was to act as a tour guide. She led the tourists to the prayer room. She showed them the pictures on the walls and explained the stories behind those. She showed the tourists how to leave a note for the priest so that he could pray for the person named on the note. Then, the tourists were free to look around and shop at the gift shop. Sylvia thought she had some time before the tourists walked in to the gift shop. She hurried to the gift shop and pushed the bookshelf aside, slipped through the door, and pushed the bookshelf back in its place. What she didn't know was that a little girl saw her do it. The little girl gasped and told her mom, who told Narina, another nun who was passing by.

Narina was shocked to learn the secret. She asked the girl to describe whom she saw. The girl described her as a tall, lean woman with beautiful green eyes. The nun thanked her. She knew it was Sylvia whom the little girl had seen.

A few hours later, when all the tourists had left, Narina told Mother Hope what the girl had seen. Mother Hope gasped. Narina was not one of Sylvia's friends. She wanted to get Sylvia in trouble. "What if she is hiding something, or worse.........someone!" she said slyly.

Mother Hope's mind was getting poisoned. "We shall spy on her tonight!" Mother Hope declared. Narina chuckled softly.

Chapter 4: A Stakeout

That night, Mother Hope and Narina did not go to bed. Mother Hope stood downstairs behind a lamp. Narina stood outside her bedroom. As midnight struck, Sylvia slipped out of her bedroom and tiptoed down the stairs to the gift shop. Narina and Mother Hope trailed close behind. They followed Sylvia through the gift shop. They saw Sylvia slide the bookshelf, open the oak wood door, and slide inside. They stood outside the door, waiting patiently while Sylvia worked on her books. Soon she got tired, blew out the candles, yawned, and walked right into Narina's trap.

"Caught you!" Narina exclaimed as Sylvia stood open-mouthed right outside the doorway.

Mother Hope was grim. "Tell us, Sylvia. What are you hiding?" she asked.

Sylvia looked down at her feet. "I can't hold it in anymore! Come in and I will show you." Sylvia burst out. As

Sylvia led them in, Narina snickered. "I have been making books." Sylvia started. She point to the table on the right, "I write and edit them here." She pointed to the table on the left. "I make the pictures and the cover here." Then Sylvia pointed to the bookshelf. "Those are all the books that I have made. I was too afraid to tell anyone or show anyone so I worked at night. But how did you find out?"

It was Narina's turn to talk. "A little girl saw you and told me." She triumphantly said, glancing at Mother Hope.

Mother Hope took no notice of her. "Sylvia, these books are beautiful! You should have told me about them. We will get them published." Mother Hope smiled.

Sylvia was overjoyed. "Oh, Mother Hope!" she said, "Thank you so much! I am truly sorry that I did not tell you!"

"You are welcome. Now, everyone back to bed!"

Yastika Singh

Chapter 5: Bestsellers

A month later, Mother Hope met with a publisher and arranged to have Sylvia's books published. Sylvia's books became bestsellers soon. When the news that Sylvia's books were bestsellers reached the nunnery, there was a huge celebration. There was music, games, and food. Everyone had fun except Narina. She pouted the whole time. Sylvia came to her. "Narina, I really want to thank you. If you had not told Mother Hope about what the girl saw, I would not have published my books. Thank you." Narina just smiled. A little while later, Sylvia went to Mother Hope and told her she wanted to do one last thing.

She asked Mother Hope if she could find the little girl's phone number. She told Mother Hope that she wanted to thank the little girl. Mother Hope went to great lengths to find the little girl's phone number. She called the number and gave the phone to Sylvia.

"Hello! My name is Sylvia and I am from the St. Stephen's Nunnery. I would like to speak to your daughter because she did a very nice thing for me and I would like to thank her."

The other end was quiet and then a small voice said, "Hello?"

"Hi! What is your name?" Sylvia asked.

"Lily," the little girl said.

"Lily, I would like to thank you. I am the nun you saw go in through the secret door. If you hadn't told the other nun, my secret would not have been exposed, and I would never have published my books. I was writing books but was too scared to tell anyone. Thank you again. I feel like we could be great friends. What do you say to dinner on Sunday?"

Lily laughed. "You're welcome! I would love to have dinner with you! Bye!"

"Bye!" Sylvia said and hung up.

Sunday came around. Lily and Sylvia had dinner at a traditional Greek restaurant. They laughed, talked, and joked around. Narina started to get along with Sylvia. Everyone was happy. Mother Hope watched it all and smiled. It was a happy nunnery!

DON'T HIDE!!!

The Working Class

~

Chapter 1: Homework over Break

"Trrriiiing!" The bell rang, indicating that the eighth period was over. "Class, your homework over the break is to go to one of your parents' workplace and write a report on what they do" said Mr. Ryan. He was the fifth grade English teacher at Lakewood Public School. It was the Friday before winter break, and all the kids were desperately waiting to get out of school. Most of the kids groaned when they heard the assignment, except one. His name was Tom Mildew. He was sleeping. He hated school so much he tuned out whatever was boring to him. As all the kids rushed out the door, Tom awoke. He picked up his things and ran after them. He met up with his best friend, Ronald. They always walked home together because they were neighbors.

"I can't believe we have homework over winter break!" Ronald complained.

Tom was suddenly alert. He asked, "What homework?"

"Come on! Sleeping again? We have to go to one of our

parents' workplaces and write a report on what they do." Ronald explained.

Tom groaned. "Great! More homework…" Tom complained.

"Race you home," Ronald said and ran off into the snow.

"Hey, wait up!" Tom shrieked and he started running, too. When they reached their houses, they were out of breath. Ronald had reached first, of course.

"Cheat!" Tom muttered, after a while.

"See ya, Thomas!" Ronald teased.

Tom grimaced. He hated being called Thomas. Tom rang the doorbell outside his house. Ronald did the same. Both doors swung open. Ronald ran inside to the warmth of his house. "Hey Mom," Tom said. He took off his shoes and stepped inside.

"Hey Tom, how was school?" Mrs. Mildew asked. "School was fine. We have English homework. We have to go to one of our parents' workplace and write a report on what they do. I was wondering if you or dad could take me to your workplace tomorrow." Tom looked up at his tall and beautiful mother.

"Sure! Daddy can take you. I have a meeting tomorrow with the other teachers." Mrs. Mildew was a teacher in another school.

"Cool! What time do I leave?" Tom asked.

"6:00 a.m. sharp!" Mrs. Mildew told Tom.

"6:00 a.m.! Are you kidding me? If he has to go that early, that is going to be the most boring part of my vacation! Agghhhhh!" Tom complained. He ran up the stairs and turned on his TV.

That night, Tom ate his dinner so slowly that he was the last one left at the dinner table. He decided he would not go to his dad's office in the morning. He went to bed feeling better.

The next morning, Tom's mom went to wake him up. Tom rolled over groggily. "What?" he asked sleepily.

"You will get your dad late for office! Come on!" Mrs. Mildew urged.

"I am not going," Tom told her.

"Oh, yes, you are!" Mrs. Mildew said, "Your father is waiting for you! Now, I better see you downstairs fully dressed with a notebook and sharpened pencil to take notes in 10 minutes. Do you hear me?"

"Yes ma'am," said Tom, his eyes lowered. Mrs. Mildew went down the stairs and Tom got out of bed. He brushed his teeth, took a quick shower, dressed, grabbed his notebook and pencil, and headed down the stairs. A bowl of oatmeal was waiting for him on the kitchen table. Tom put some walnuts and raisins in his oatmeal and started to eat. His mom put a bag next to him.

"This has your lunch, water, and a book for you to read in case you get bored," she told him.

"Which will be the whole time," he muttered.

"Ready to go, son?" called out Mr. Mildew, standing at the door.

"Yeah, whatever," Tom said unenthusiastically.

Mr. Mildew was a fraud detector. He monitored people's credit card transactions and tracked people who stole credit card information. "Let's go," he said. Tom rolled his eyes. He finished his oatmeal and went to the car. "Bye, honey!" Mrs. Mildew said to Mr. Mildew. Mr. Mildew waved to his wife and hopped into his car. He buckled up and started driving.

"We are going to have a blast," Mr. Mildew told Tom.

"In your dreams," Tom said to himself.

"Excuse me?" Mr. Mildew asked suspiciously.

"Nothing," Tom said quickly.

They drove for forty minutes, Mr. Mildew talking the

whole time. Finally, their car pulled into a parking space in front of a huge glass building. "This is where you work?" Tom asked, suddenly interested.

"Sure is", his dad replied. The two of them got out of the car and walked towards the building. As they entered the building, Tom saw a man sitting at a large desk. Mr. Mildew was used to this, of course. "Tom, meet Mr. Rodda, the desk manager. Mr. Rodda, my son, Tom," Mr. Mildew introduced Tom and Mr. Rodda, and then went on to explain to Mr. Rodda why he had brought his son along.

"Hi there, kid. Your dad has a very important job. You will love it." Mr. Rodda told Tom.

"If I even stay awake," Tom said.

"What do you mean, son? You have been muttering things all morning. What's going on?" Mr. Mildew questioned.

"Nothing, let's just get on with this. I am going to be bored to death, anyway." Tom replied.

"Well, if you feel that way, why are you here?" Mr. Mildew asked.

"It is because of a stupid school project. Where do we go?" Tom asked. Mr. Mildew led the way. They entered an elevator, and Mr. Mildew pressed the button for the third floor. The doors closed and the elevator started to move. There was an awkward silence between Mr. Mildew and Tom. Before Tom could say anything to ease the situation, the doors opened. Mr. Mildew walked out into a long hallway with several mirrors and Tom followed. He followed his dad into a large room that had a large desk, a computer, chairs and a whiteboard with many markers. "Nice room," Tom commented.

"Thanks" Mr. Mildew said, looking at his desk.

Chapter 2: A Discovery

"What do you do all day?" Tom asked, trying to show some interest.

"Well, you know that I am a fraud detector, right?" Mr. Mildew asked. Tom nodded and got out his notebook and pencil. "I monitor people's credit card transactions and detect fraud. If I find anything suspicious, I investigate the fraud and gather evidence. So, basically, I am an expert at fraud detection," said Mr. Mildew. Tom wrote slowly. He began to pay more attention with every word.

"Wow, that's pretty cool! Can you tell me about how you investigate fraud?" Tom asked after a while.

"Well, I look at the last use of a credit card, and then I interview people who have a possible motive. It is hard but fun." Tom started to scribble furiously.

"How much time does it take you to investigate a case?" Tom asked.

"Well, it could take days, weeks, or even months depending on how well the thief disguises himself or herself," Mr. Mildew said. He began to sense Tom's interest but acted cool. Tom asked him questions for about an hour until Mr. Mildew had to get back to his work. Tom read the book his mother had packed for him. He thought about how his father worked all day. No recess, no throwing paper airplanes. His father did all this for his family. He thought about how maybe, just somehow, school could be fun if he paid attention. Tom stood up and silently resolved to pay attention in school and never let his parents down.

"Hey, Tommy, come here. This is the action of my day," Mr. Mildew beckoned Tom.

Tom ran over, saying, "Okay. I am ready for it."

"Okay, so I just detected a fraud. Someone stole five thousand dollars from a rich man named Devone La Souista. Let's see…The credit card was last used in a beauty shop. Okay, I am not questioning this guy or his weird beauty shopping hobbies." Tom laughed. "Let's get a list of the beauty shop's employees" Mr. Mildew said. With a click of a button, Mr. Mildew was examining employees' profiles. "Hey, I've seen this man before. He is a known criminal. They call him the *Disappearing Act* because he stays in one place for a while and then suddenly disappears. But, seriously, a beauty shop? It is time for some action. First, I have to call the bank and then the police," Mr. Mildew said as sure as an army general. He picked up his telephone and dialed a few numbers. "Hello, we have detected a fraud. The victim is Devone La Souista and the culprit is probably the *Disappearing Act*." He started. After a minute or two, he hung up and then he called the police and told them the story. He was on the phone for a few minutes, discussing the plan to catch the thief. After a while, Mr. Mildew put down the phone and said, "Let's do some more investigating." Tom looked over his dad's shoulder at the computer. Mr. Mildew checked the profiles of the employees at *Minnie's Beauty Appliances*, the shop where the *Disappearing Act* worked. He scrolled to the bottom. He clicked on the *Disappearing Act's* image. He continued clicking on links and logging into web sites, collecting information about the *Disappearing Act*.

"Let me guess, you are going to help the police a little by showing the *Disappearing Act's* most likely whereabouts?" Tom asked.

"Sure am. You're pretty good at this, Tom. I'm really glad you came". Mr. Mildew said.

"I'm glad I came, too" Tom replied.

Chapter 3: An act of inspiration

By that time, Mr. Mildew and Tom were hungry. "Let's go have some lunch. I know a great noodle place across the street."

"Okay, let's go. I'm starving," Tom said. They started to leave when Mr. Mildew got a text message on his phone.

"Excuse me for a second". Mr. Mildew took out his phone and checked the message. "No, no, no, no, no! It happened! It had to happen!" Mr. Mildew cried.

"What, what happened?" Tom asked frantically.

"Someone hacked into our central computer and shut down our network. We can't do anything. Our reputation will be ruined. I should've known. The *Disappearing Act* detected that we were trying to find him, and shut our network down. Did I tell you that he is a computer hacker, too? We have a conference today to answer questions. I have to calm people down and think of a solution." Mr. Mildew said and sat down in a swivel chair.

"I'm sure you will find a solution," Tom said.

"You know what? Don't worry about it. I'll think of something. I just need some inspiration. Let's go eat some noodles," Mr. Mildew said, trying to sound cheerful. The two of them walked out of the building quietly. Tom could sense that Mr. Mildew was depressed. They walked across the street and into a restaurant called "Flavor China". They walked to the counter where a cheerful man greeted them.

"Good afternoon, Mr. Mildew. Spicy Chicken special? Extra spicy as usual? Oh and who is this young man?" the man asked.

"Hi Monty, how are you? Tom, this is Monty. We are great friends. Monty, my son, Tom," Mr. Mildew introduced them.

"Pleasure to meet you, Tom," Monty said.

"It's nice to meet you, too!" Tom exclaimed.

Monty looked at Mr. Mildew's face for a while. "You are stressed out about something, Mr. Mildew. Tell me what it is," Monty said.

"That's you, Monty, always able to figure someone out. Work problems, that is all," Mr. Mildew said with a sigh.

"Ah, I hear you" Monty replied. Tom suddenly went behind the counter towards Monty. He beckoned him to bend down. Monty looked at him suspiciously but obliged. Tom whispered something in his ear. When he finished, Monty laughed and Mr. Mildew raised an eyebrow. Suddenly Monty and Tom began acting out a funny scene.

"Welcome to Tom's magic. The pocket trick will be witnessed now," Tom recited. "Come here, young man, and close your eyes. Then, spin around in a circle," Tom told Monty. Monty obeyed. Tom secretly grabbed his wallet. "Now stop and check your pocket" Tom said. Monty obeyed.

"It's magic! My wallet, it is gone!" Monty exclaimed. Mr. Mildew laughed heartily. Tom gave back Monty's wallet and they both bowed.

"Feel any better?" Tom asked his father.

"Yes, thanks" Mr. Mildew answered. They paid for lunch and as they were leaving, they waved goodbye to Monty.

They took their food and went back to Mr. Mildew's office. When they reached the room, they started to eat. "This is delicious," Tom said but Mr. Mildew was in deep thought. They finished their food in silence.

"It's time for the conference. Let us go to the conference room. You have to be very quiet if you want to go inside," Mr. Mildew said.

"Okay, I will be quiet. Good luck, dad!" Tom tried to encourage his father. It seemed to work. Mr. Mildew and

Tom went down the hallway of mirrors and then stopped at a glass revolving door. They entered the room and sat down at a very long table. Men and women were seated at the other chairs. Suddenly, Mr. Mildew stood up. Everyone fell silent.

"This conference is about finding a solution to our huge problem. As you all know, one of the criminals, probably the *Disappearing Act...*" started Mr. Mildew. Everyone gasped and whispered. "As I was saying, the criminal hacked into our network and shut down our entire network. I really don't have a plan to fix this, so I am open to suggestions." People started to groan and yawn. Then, Mr. Mildew remembered Tom's act. "Wait. That's it! I have an idea," he said. "We have to trick the criminal." Just then, the computer monitor in front of him beeped and displayed an alert. The same alert was displayed on all the computers. This could only mean one thing. Someone was logged in to the central computer. That is why the network was back on and the alert was displaying on all the computers. The criminal must be there now. Mr. Mildew remembered that the central computer was in a hotel room on forty-second Street to avoid attention. "We have to tell the police to send some officers to the Central Hotel on forty-second Street. I will go, too. Carl, call the police and tell them everything. Dina, call the head of Cyber Security and ask for their best technician to be on standby. Melanie, call the bank and assure them that everything will be okay. Tom, come with me." Mr. Mildew had found his confidence back. He seemed to be in complete control of the situation. As Tom saw everyone carry out his father's orders, he was very impressed.

Chapter 4: The Capture

Mr. Mildew and Tom got into their car and drove to forty-second Street. The police were already there. A policewoman was disguised as a maid. Mr. Mildew and Tom went into the building with the "maid". They went to the hotel room in which the central computer was kept. They tried to open the door slowly but it was locked. The policewoman knocked on the door.

"Who is it?" a gruff voice asked.

"Room Service," the fake maid called. She pulled out handcuffs. Tom and Mr. Mildew hid out of sight.

The door opened slightly and a man asked, "I don't remember ordering anything but can I have some popcorn?"

"Oh you can have some popcorn alright... in jail!" the maid exclaimed. And as swift as a leopard she swung the man around and handcuffed his hands. Mr. Mildew rushed in and took control of the central computer.

"That was awesome!" Tom admired the policewoman's work.

"Thanks, kid" the policewoman said and took the man away.

Chapter 5: Tom's Apology

"Great job, Dad," Tom congratulated Mr. Mildew.

"Thanks, son, I wouldn't have thought of this idea if you hadn't put up your act".

Tom laughed. "Hey listen, dad! I am really sorry I said those mean things this morning. Your job is awesome – just like you are!" Tom apologized.

"It is okay, Tom. And remember, it is not only me that works all day. Every parent works hard for their kids and family."

"Thanks dad! Let's go home now!" Tom said cheerfully. They got into their car and drove home. That night, Mrs. Mildew asked Tom how his day was.

"It was the best day I ever had. And thanks mom, for supporting our family."

Mrs. Mildew laughed. "You are welcome. Now go to bed."

A week later, school reopened. Tom was the first one to present his English project. "My dad detects frauds by monitoring people's credit card transactions. He tracks criminals and runs online investigations. He sits all day in front of a computer just so that our families are safe. He doesn't have recess or free time. All parents do this for their kids. It is great to know that they are there for you. And all of us should be thankful for that." Tom finished.

He got an A+ for his project. From that day onwards, Tom always did well in school. He stayed true to his resolution and never took advantage of his parents.

APPRECIATE WHAT PEOPLE DO FOR YOU!!!

Yastika Singh

About the Author

Yastika Singh is a curious ten year old who lives in a small town named Woodland Park in New Jersey. She wrote her first e-book titled "Random Harvest" when she was just seven years old. Yastika takes her everyday experiences and turns them into beautiful works of art by creating exceptional characters and abundant details. Her hobbies are gymnastics and chess. In her spare time, she is always working on new ideas, new ways of doing things.

She dreams of becoming an author, a renowned gymnast, a chess champion, an FBI agent, and a lawyer. Sky is the limit for this talented youngster.

Through this book, she tries to get characters to follow their dreams and not give up, just like she does. This book is her dream – come true.